Captain

★AWESOME

AND THE
MISSING
ELEPHANTS

By STAN KIRBY

Illustrated by GEORGE O'CONNOR

LITTLE SIMON

New York   London   Toronto   Sydney   New Delhi

 LITTLE SIMON

An imprint of Simon & Schuster Children's Publishing Division • 1230 Avenue of the Americas, New York, New York 10020 • Copyright © 2014 by Simon & Schuster, Inc. All rights reserved, including the right of reproduction in whole or in part in any form. LITTLE SIMON is a registered trademark of Simon & Schuster, Inc., and associated colophon is a trademark of Simon & Schuster, Inc. For information about special discounts for bulk purchases, please contact Simon & Schuster Special Sales at 1-866-506-1949 or business@simonandschuster.com. The Simon & Schuster Speakers Bureau can bring authors to your live event. For more information or to book an event contact the Simon & Schuster Speakers Bureau at 1-866-248-3049 or visit our website at www.simonspeakers.com. Designed by Jay Colvin. Manufactured in the United States of America 1015 MTN
10 9 8 7 6 5 4
Library of Congress Cataloging-in-Publication Data
Kirby, Stan. Captain Awesome and the missing elephant / by Stan Kirby ; illustrated by George O'Connor. — First edition. pages cm. — (Captain Awesome ; #10) Summary: "On a class field trip to the Sunnyview Memorial Zoo, Eugene McGillicudy's favorite animals—the elephants—are missing! Is Randy the tour guide really the evil Raging Radonkey, trying to ruin the field trip? Can the Sunnyview Superhero Squad save the day and find the elephants?" — Provided by publisher. [1. Superheroes—Fiction. 2. School field trips—Fiction. 3. Lost and found possessions—Fiction. 4. Elephants—Fiction. 5. Zoos—Fiction.] I. O'Connor, George, illustrator. II. Title. PZ7.K633529Cad 2014 [E] —dc23 2013001072
ISBN 978-1-4424-8994-3 (pbk)
ISBN 978-1-4424-8995-0 (hc)
ISBN 978-1-4424-8996-7 (eBook)

Table of Contents

CHAPTER 1

Tomorrow Is the Day!

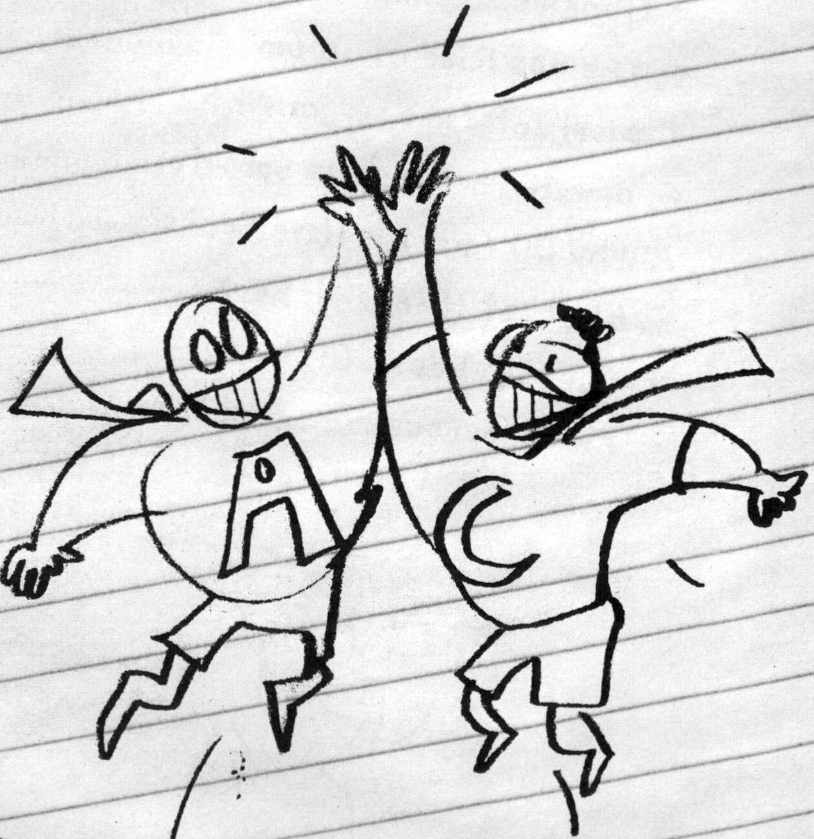

By Eugene

Two words:
FIELD!
TRIP!

What? Oh! **FIELD TRIP!**

Aside from "no homework," are there two greater words in the history of school? The words "field" and "trip" together promise a day of fun, a day away from school, and a day where anything can happen.

Those words are the chocolate

and peanut butter of education.

And for Eugene, this chocolate-y, peanut-butter-y, field-trippy goodness was all going to happen tomorrow.

"Don't forget to bring your permission slips, class," said Ms. Beasley, "or you won't be going to the zoo."

Eugene McGillicudy wouldn't miss a field trip any more than he'd miss New Comic Book Day at the comic book store. That's because the Sunnyview Memorial Zoo had the greatest animals in the world.

"Just think of it, Charlie," Eugene said to his best friend, Charlie Thomas Jones. "Lions with razor-sharp laser claws!"

"And tigers with stripes of invisibility!" Charlie added.

"And hippopom . . . hippotap . . . um . . . *hippos*, with their giant mud-covered butts of stinky stink,"Eugene said.

"And don't forget the elephants!" Charlie said. "With their supertrunk powers and huge, flappy ears that can whip up the Whistling Wind of Seven Cyclones!"

"That's right!" Eugene agreed. "*Especially* elephants."

AWESOME!

Eugene thought of that time in

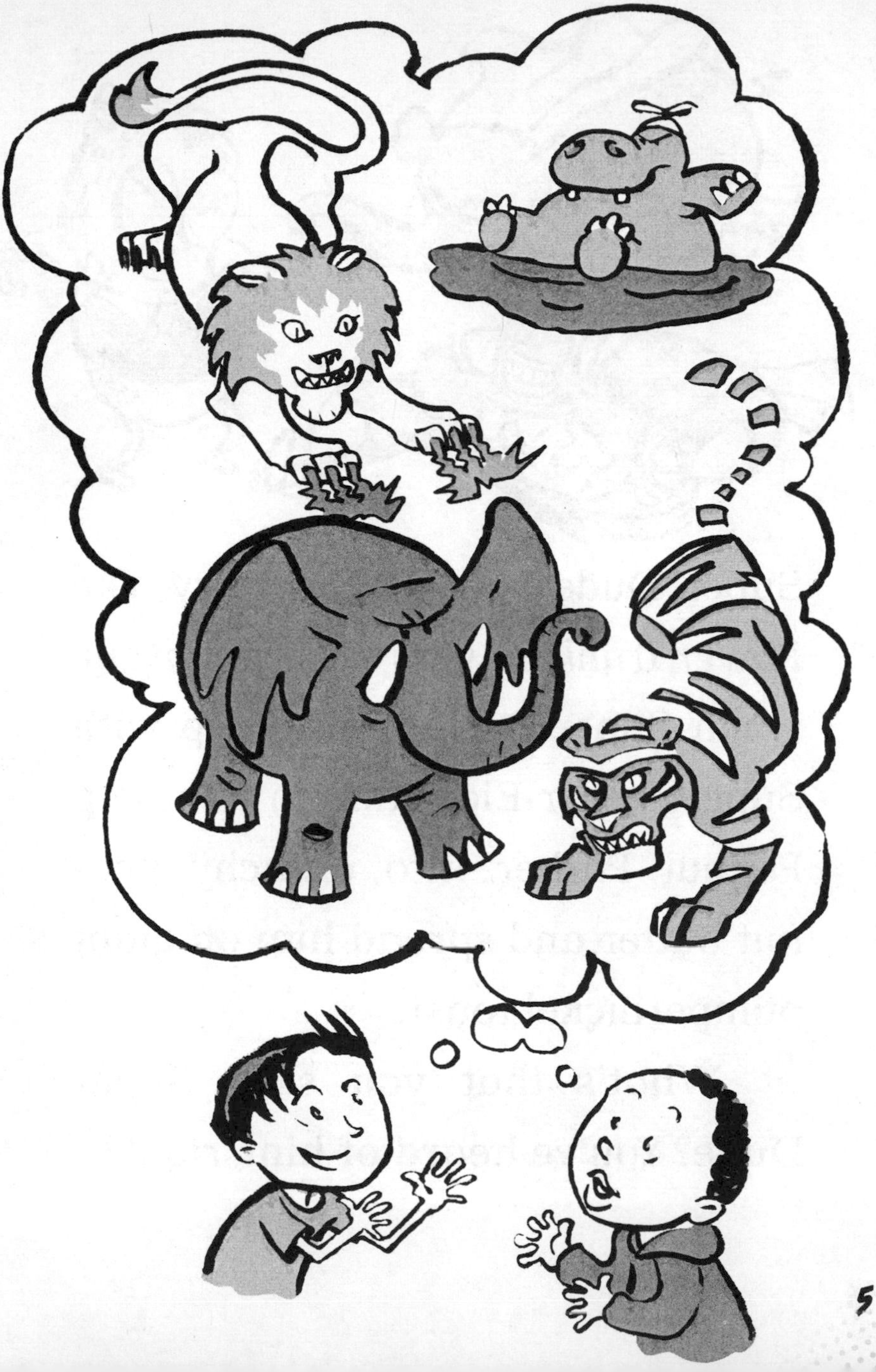

Super Dude No. 18, the story *The Power Trunk Powers of Elephantom*, when Super Dude teamed up with Super Duper Elephantom to stomp Peanut Parker into crunchy peanut butter and spread him on giant pumpernickel toast.

What's that you say? Super Dude? You've heard of him, right?

WHAT?

You mean you don't know the answer to the easiest question in the *Easy Question Book of Easy Questions*?

Question one: WHO IS SUPER DUDE?

Answer: Super Dude is the world's greatest superhero— he's greater than Mr. Greatman and more rad than King Power Rad, the really powerful leader of Radsylvania. Super Dude is the superhero who once knocked the stuffing out of the evil Teddy Bearenstein and dried up the deadly Spitballer before he could fire his lava spit from his Ultra Plastic Straw of Evil.

But Super Dude was more than a true hero and Eugene's favorite of all time. He was the reason Eugene became Sunnyview's first and most awesome superhero. That's right. Eugene had a secret identity: He was: CAPTAIN AWESOME!

MI-TEE!

It's true. Sunnyview had its very own superhero! And not just one, either.

There was . . . ANOTHER!

Charlie was the superhero Nacho Cheese Man—the only hero with the power of canned cheese!

CHEESY YO!

Along with their class's superpet hamster, Turbo, Eugene and Charlie formed the Sunnyview Superhero Squad to stop the eviling of bad guys and to keep Sunnyview safe.

But what happened when they discovered that their neighbor Sally Williams was also a "Keep

Sunnyview Safe" superhero called Supersonic Sal? Well, she was asked to join the group too!

Together these four heroes would put badness in its place! And that place would be . . . far away from all goodness.

CHAPTER 2

Tricky Little Miss Stinky Pinky

By Eugene

Ring!

The school bell was the greatest sound in the world that wasn't
the sound of Super Dude smacking
evil or the opening of a new bag of
potato chips. Eugene shot out of
his desk, ran to his cubby, slipped
and fell *into* his cubby, grabbed his
backpack, and headed for the door.

"Forget anything, puke-Gene?"

Eugene froze. He knew that

high-pitched screech. It could only
be one of three things:

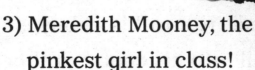

1) Angry Monkey
   Man trying to steal
   his lunch!
2) The Dreaded
   Opera Boy
   and his solo of
   doom!
3) Meredith Mooney, the
   pinkest girl in class!

"My! Me! Mine! Meredith!"
Eugene said. "What do *you* want?"

Meredith stood in the doorway, the pink sleeves on her arms folded across her pink shirt. The pink ribbons in her hair were as big as helicopter blades. Eugene hoped they'd start spinning and carry her away.

"Aren't you forgetting your permission slip?" she asked.

Eugene reached into his pocket and pulled out . . . nothing.

NO!

He reached into all his pockets and pulled out more nothing.

Oh no! Eugene thought. *It's gone!*

Eugene turned back to his desk. Empty! He turned back around to Meredith, but she was no longer the pink classmate he saw: She was Little Miss Stinky Pinky, Captain Awesome's most awful enemy. His permission slip dangled from her evil fingers.

She was determined to keep the mighty Captain Awesome from the

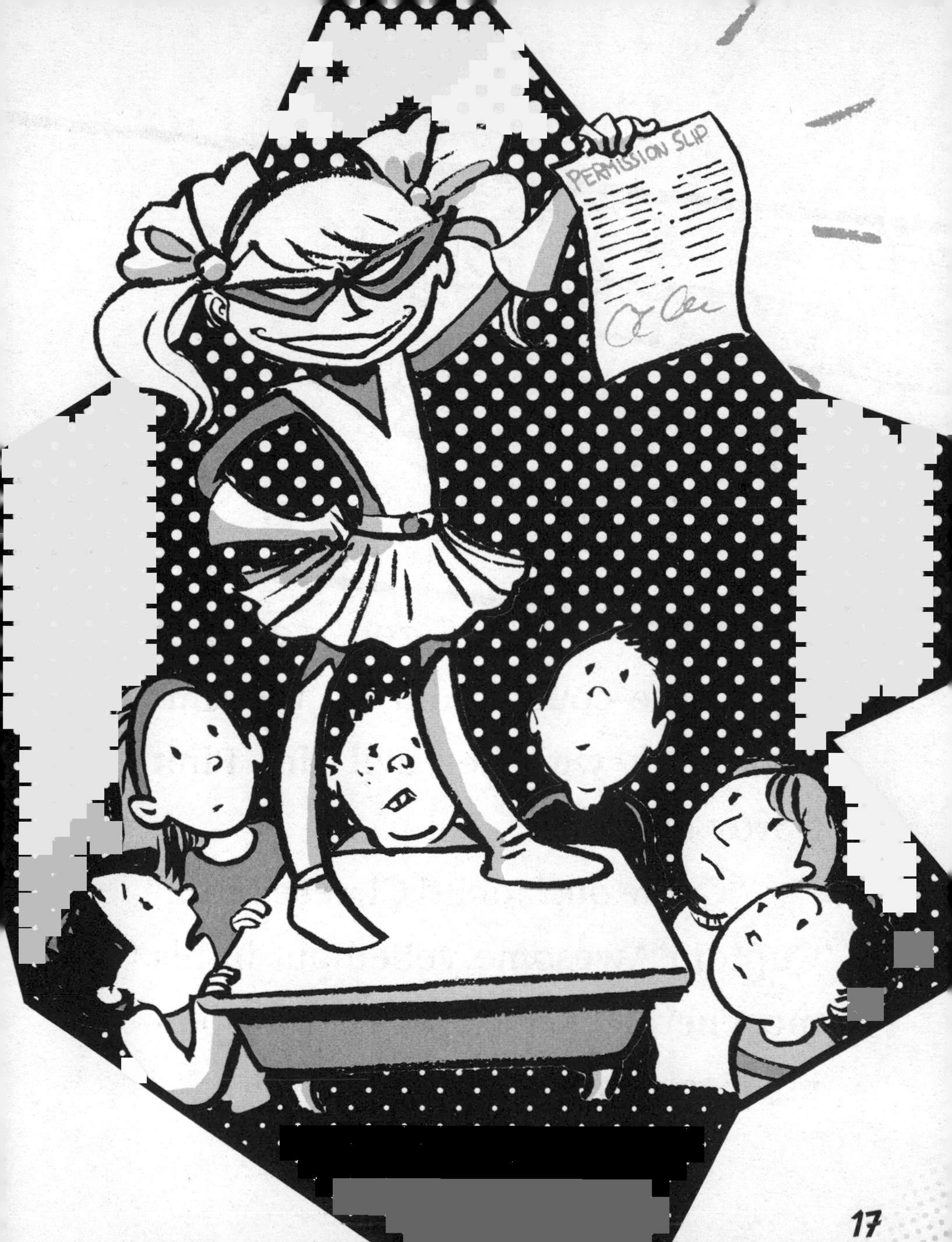
PERMISSION SLIP

[redacted]

zoo so that
she could paint all the animals pink with her evil Hot Pink
Spray Paint!

"Come on, Nacho Cheese Man!"
Captain Awesome yelled out in his
most heroic voice. "Let's get my permission slip back! MI-TEE!"

"Cheesy yo!" cried Nacho Cheese Man. He pulled a spray can of spicy nacho cheese from his cheese bag.

The danger-stopping dynamos raced through the doorway and into the evil pink lair of Little Miss Stinky Pinky!

She screamed and ran away.

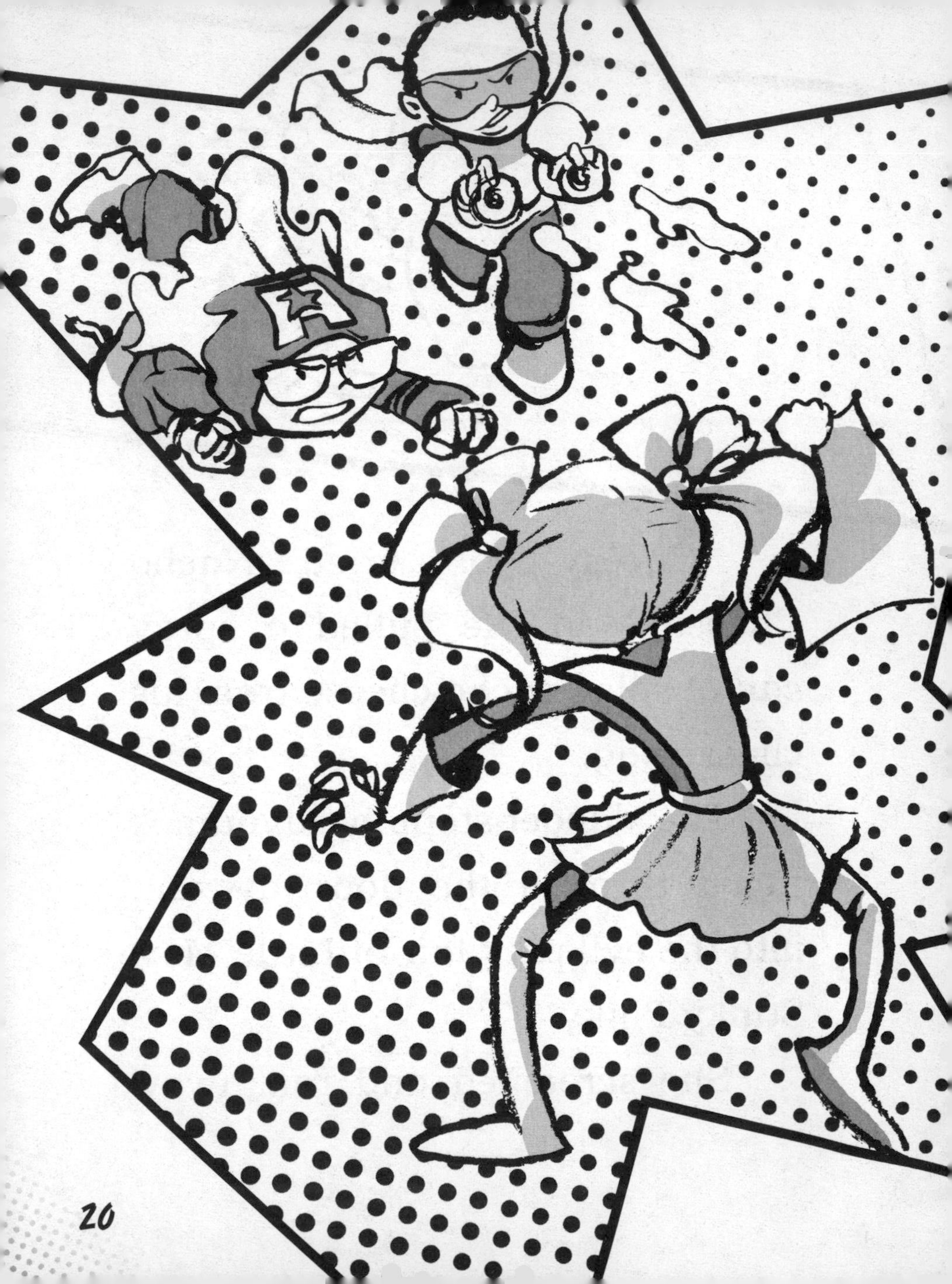

Nacho Cheese Man blasted a spray of cheese at her feet, but his aim was off and he painted a cheese smile on a nearby locker.

ZOOM!

A blur whooshed past Captain Awesome and Nacho Cheese Man. It was Supersonic Sal!

She ran fast circles around
Little Miss Stinky Pinky, who grew
dizzier and dizzier trying to watch
Sunnyview's fastest hero.

"What are you doing? Stop!
I'm . . ." Little Miss Stinky Pinky
spun around and around.

Captain Awesome reached
over and grabbed the permission

slip from Little Miss Stinky Pinky's fingers.

"Mission accomplished!" he yelled heroically.

Then the three heroes walked triumphantly out of Little Miss Stinky Pinky's lair of evil. The field trip was saved!

CHAPTER 3

Superheroes Get Their Powers from Cookies

By
Eugene

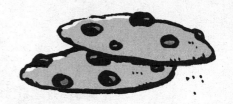

"**M**mph." Eugene's mouth was stuffed with chocolate-chip cookies.

"Mmph."Charlie tried to answer, but his mouth was also stuffed with chocolate-chip cookies.

Sally heroically held her cookie in the air. "By the authority and power of these chocolate-chip cookies, I call this meeting of the Sunnyview Superhero Squad to

order." Then she took a bite.

Eugene, Charlie, and Sally had assembled after school in the Sunnyview Superhero Squad's secret headquarters: the tree house in Eugene's backyard.

Eugene gulped down the last of his cookie. "The first item on our list of items is item number one."

"I know that one: Eat another one of your mom's homemade cookies!" Charlie popped another cookie into his mouth. He handed one to Sally.

Who am I to argue with fresh-baked genius? Eugene thought.

Eugene helped himself to two more. He chewed them with a big smile and unrolled a giant sheet of

paper across the Official Floor of the Sunnyview Superhero Squad Clubhouse. "Item number two: this map of the zoo."

"Hmm, where is the Elephant Habitat?" Sally asked.

"Right here, past the rhinos, giraffes, and . . . pink flamingos,"

Eugene pointed out, almost gagging when he said the word "pink."

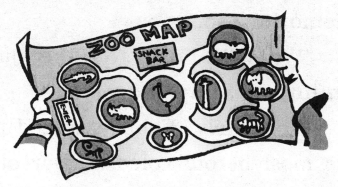

He marked the Elephant Habitat with a big red X.

There was one last item on the checklist: evil.

"What about evil?" Charlie asked.

"There is always evil!" Eugene announced. "And there could even be evil at a place as wonderful and awesome as the Sunnyview Memorial Zoo."

"We will have to take our uniforms," Sally suggested.

"Absolutely," Eugene agreed in his most heroic voice. "If our old enemies hatch a plot of evil, we can't wait for the bus to take us back to school so that we can walk home, get our uniforms, and have my mom drive us back to the zoo."

That's when the heroes heard the growl.

"Grrrrrrrrrrrrr . . ."

That growl meant trouble.

"Grrrrrrrrrrrr . . ."

It was the sound of their four-legged enemy.

"Mr. Drools!" Eugene cried. "He's been listening to every word!"

"He knows our plans!" Charlie exclaimed.

"He'll try to stop us from getting to the zoo!" Sally yelled.

And Mr. Drools would try to do just that. He was the most slobberingest monster ever to be unleashed from the Howling Paw Nebula. He could wake up sleepy people around the galaxy with his Noisy Bark of Loudness, and then destroy them with his Drool of Destruction and his Double-Dog

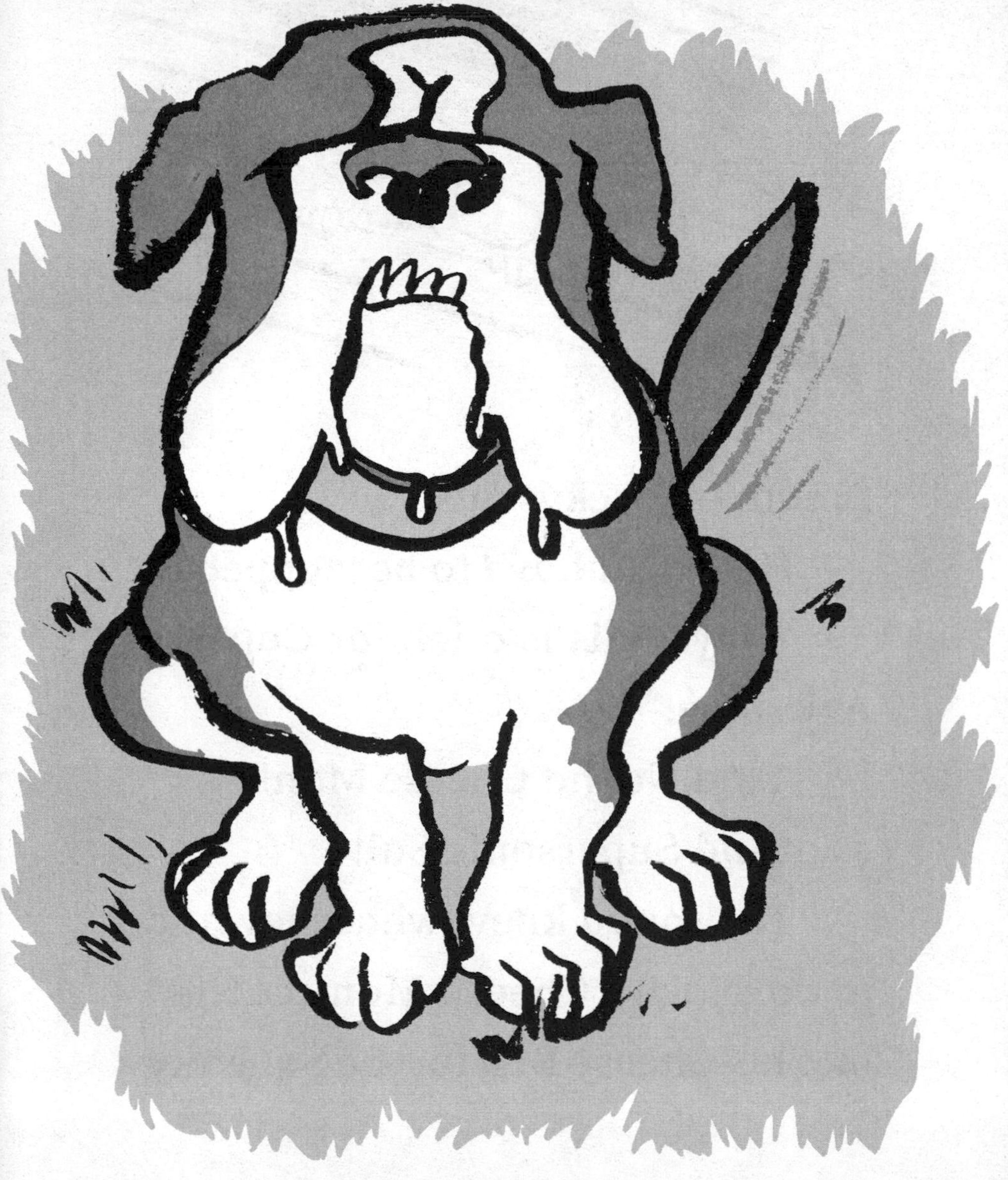

Breath of Yucky-Yuck.

He would have to be stopped.

"Guys, this is a job for Captain Awesome!"

"And Nacho Cheese Man!"

"And Supersonic Sal!"

The squad knew what they had to do. Nacho Cheese Man reached into his Cheese Bag for the Squeaky

Squeezo toy that no dog could resist.

"Cheesy-NO!" Nacho Cheese Man said with a gasp.

It was gone. They'd forgotten to refill the bag with a new Squeezo toy after their last battle with Mr. Drools.

"We are totally doomed," Nacho Cheese Man said doomfully.

"No worries," Supersonic Sal replied. "We have: Plan B!"

Captain Awesome opened up the Storage Box of Awesomeness and picked up the Throwing Stick of Tossing. It was crafted from a branch of the finest oak tree that had been struck by a lightning blast from Lightning Lady.

"This is sure to stop him," Supersonic Sal said without any doom in her voice.

Captain Awesome pulled back his arm and swung the Throwing Stick through the air.

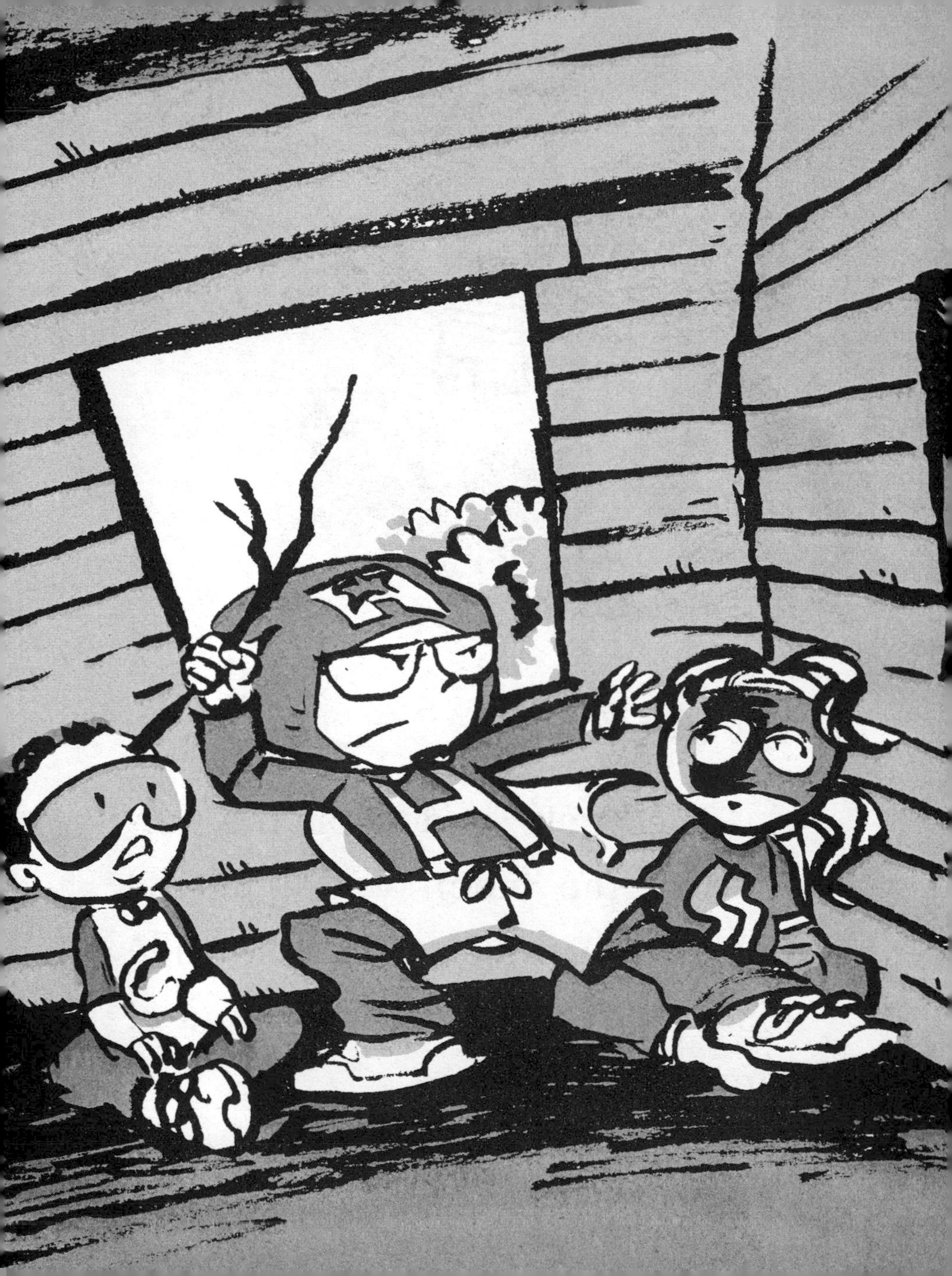

The stick landed on the sur-
face of the moon and bounced
over Mr. Drools's head. It then
disappeared into a large cloud of
Moon Fog.

"Fetch!" Captain Awesome yelled to Mr. Drools. The mighty beast of evil looked at Captain Awesome, Nacho Cheese Man, and Supersonic Sal, but he could not ignore the Throwing Stick.

His drooly tongue flopped out of his mouth. He turned and ran after the stick, disappearing into fog. He would not be seen again for several days.

CHAPTER 4

The Bus Ride of Doom!

BY
Eugene

Run!

Eager to get good seats on the bus, Eugene, Charlie, and Sally raced to school the next morning.

"Okay, class!" Ms. Beasley announced, tapping her clipboard. "I've got your seat assignments right here."

Seat assignments? Assigned seats? Eugene thought it sounded like the worst idea since fried okra.

"Starting at the front of the bus, every one of you will be sitting in alphabetical order."

PUKE!

Alphabetical order was even worse! That was the worst idea since boy-girl-boy-girl!

I don't even keep my Super Dude Power Cards in alphabetical order, Eugene thought.

"Howard Adams and Neal Chaykin, you're first." Ms. Beasley pointed to the bus.

Howard and Neal climbed up the bus steps. Eugene's mind raced through the last names of his classmates: Gil Ditko, Wilma Eisner, Mike Flinch, Charlie Thomas Jones, Stan Kirby Jr., Eugene McGillicudy, Meredith Mooney . . .

McGillicudy . . . Mooney. Mooney?
MEREDITH Mooney?

NOOOOO!

"But Ms. Beasley! This can't be!" Eugene cried. "There isn't anyone between Meredith and me!"

"That's right, Eugene. That's what alphabetical order means."

She read the names, and the students climbed onto the bus to take their seats. Eugene headed toward his seat like it was full of electric eels.

"Why, look who's here. It's Don't-gene," the pink princess said as Eugene slumped into his seat and buckled up.

"Good-bye, Charlie. Good-bye, Sally," he said sadly. He felt like Super Dude in Super Dude No. 7, when Super Dude was forced to eat Radioactive Spam by Lord Shallot, the Evil Onion King.

"Good luck, Eugene," Charlie called.

"See you at the zoo!" Sally said as she walked by.

Eugene slouched. He tried to stare out the window, but it was blocked by Meredith's big pink bows.

She pulled out her music player and turned it up to level nine. Horrible music screeched out from her earphones. It sounded like the kind of music that unicorns would play at a fairy-tale dance party.

"Isn't this a great song?" Meredith asked, yelling over the

sound of the music in her ears. "It's Girly Girl and the Girly Girls. I could listen to them all day long."

I couldn't, thought Eugene. *It's going to turn my brain into brain jelly that's going to ooze out of my ears!*

Suddenly Eugene realized the horrible truth. . . .

Little Miss Stinky Pinky had already tried to steal his permission slip. And now she was trying to melt his brain! She'd do anything to keep him from going to the zoo!

Eugene gave the secret sign to Charlie—two claps, a double finger snap, and a high-pitched whistle.

But Charlie was too busy squirting jalapeño cheese into his mouth. And Sally was taking pictures through the window.

Eugene was alone. He'd have to face Little Miss Stinky Pinky all on his own!

"Your Stinky Pinky Ear Blaster shall blast no more ears, Little Miss Stinky Pinky!" Captain Awesome cried.

Captain Awesome leaped from his seat and grabbed Little

Miss Stinky Pinky's music player. The volume button would soon be under the control of his MI-TEE thumb!

"Evil electrical devices shall be turned off!" he yelled.

"Ms. Beasley!" Miss Stinky Pinky cried out. "He's doing it again!"

Before Ms. Beasley had time to ask the questions "Who?" and "What?" Captain Awesome presented her with the music player.

"The rules have always said 'No music on the bus,' ma'am," Captain Awesome told the teacher.

"That's right, er . . . Captain Awesome," Ms. Beasley said.

Captain Awesome walked back to his seat and smiled at the pouty Little Miss Stinky Pinky. Another dose of bus justice had been served.

CHAPTER 5

Elephant Time . . . or Not

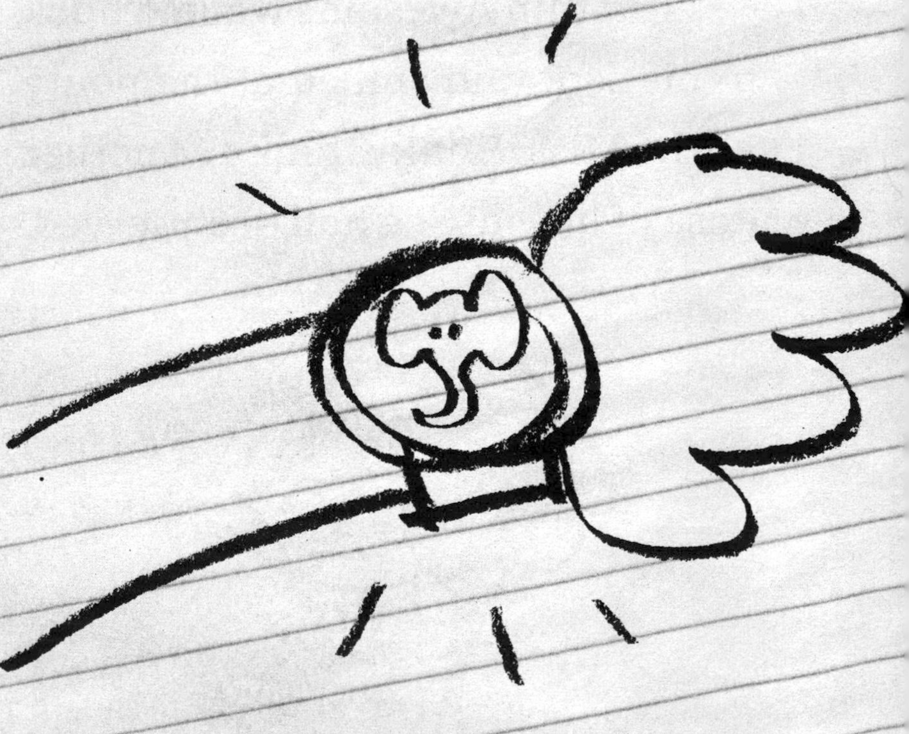

By Eugene

"**H**i, everybody! I'm Randy. And welcome to the Sunnyview Memorial Zoo!"

As the class unloaded from the bus, they were greeted by Randy, the Junior Assistant Zookeeper.

"Hi, Randy!" everyone said.

"I'll be your tour guide here today," Randy told them. "We have lots of exciting things to show you— including new baby penguins!"

"What about the elephants? When can we see Earth's coolest, awesomest creatures?" Eugene asked.

Randy turned and led the group past the sign that pointed to the rhinoceroses. "Our elephants have been a little shy lately," he

said. "We might not have enough time to see any."

NO ELEPHANTS?

Eugene was shocked. *Going to the zoo and not seeing any elephants is like going to the movies and not getting any popcorn!* he thought.

"Did you guys hear what he said?" Sally stepped between Eugene and Charlie. "Randy's up to no good."

Eugene nodded. "Randy, if that's his real name, is taking us

away from the Elephant Habitat!" he proclaimed. "He doesn't want us to see them . . . but why?"

But that question would have to wait. Randy had brought them to the Rhino Roundabout. Despite their horn of terror, the big gray beasts were plant-eaters and they wandered around the roundabout nibbling anything green.

"These are our rhinoceroses, Rupert and Rhonda," Randy said. "Aren't they magnificent?"

If only you rhinos could talk, Eugene thought. *I bet you know why Randy is trying to keep us from seeing the elephants.*

"Next stop: Lion Lounge, where you'll see the first lion born in our zoo! After that, it's Grizzly Bear Jamboree, the Monkey Mansion, and then the animals I know *someone* can't wait to see . . ."

Eugene held his breath. *Could it be . . . ?*

"Pink Flamingo Pond!" Randy announced.

"Oh yeah!" Meredith cheered and jumped up and down like a big pink jelly bean.

"I think I'm gonna barf." Eugene held his stomach.

CHAPTER 6

Beware the Brussels Sprouter!

By
Eugene

Even though they had to watch dorky pink birds standing in water for what seemed like a billion years while Meredith giggled happily, somehow Eugene did not barf all over himself. Or anyone else. And that was a very good thing because it was time for lunch, and eating at the zoo cafeteria was even better than eating a corn dog on a stick!

"No school cafeteria food for

us on *this* day!" Eugene said.

"We get animal-shaped chicken nuggets! And animal-shaped tater tots!" Charlie eagerly listed. "And best of all . . ."

"Chocolate milk with a straw shaped like an elephant's trunk!" both boys cheered together.

"This is going to be the best

lunch EVER!"Eugene added as they marched behind Randy toward the zoo cafeteria . . . and then past the zoo cafeteria? Eugene's jaw dropped as Randy walked past the animal-shaped chicken nuggets, the taters, and even the chocolate milk with elephant-trunk straws. Randy walked past everything and led the entire class to . . .

"The Brussels Sprouts Café?!" Eugene and Charlie said at the same time, gasping in horror.

GROSS!

"Yep! This is where we take *all* the school field trips," Randy said proudly. "This place is a *lot* healthier than the zoo cafeteria."

Randy held the door open and the class sadly marched toward the disgrace of steamed vegetables and sugar-free apple juice. Jake Story

let out a small whimper and it even looked as if Jane Romita was about to cry.

The moment the smell of roasted brussels sprouts attacked Eugene's nose, he grabbed Charlie and pulled him into the boys' bathroom.

"Do you know where we are?!"
Eugene asked urgently.

Charlie looked around. "In the
boys' bathroom at the Sunnyview
Memorial Zoo?"

"No! Randy's taken us to the secret food mines of the Brussels Sprouter!" Eugene explained.

"What?! No!" Charlie said, gasping. "And I thought this was just a normal bathroom."

"There's *nothing* 'normal' about Brussels sprouts!" Eugene cried. "Looks like this is a job for the forces of goodness and those who fight for a yummy lunch!"

ZIP!
UNFOLD!
CAPES!

The two boys pulled out their superhero costumes and transformed into the terrific twosome known as . . .

CAPTAIN AWESOME and NACHO CHEESE MAN!

"I'll not be tricked by your trickery, trickster!" Captain Awesome called out to Randy as he raced from the bathroom with Nacho

Cheese Man. "I know you're lead-
ing us into the lair of the sinister
Brussels Sprouter!"

"Brussels Sprouter?" Randy
looked around, confused. "That's
just our cook, Lewis."

Lewis carried a tray of freshly steamed vegetables. He was dressed in an apron with zebra stripes, and he wore a hat that looked like a zebra head. He waved to the kids.

"Boiled carrots?! He knows my carroty weakness!" Nacho Cheese

Man gagged, falling to his knees. "Growing . . . weak . . ."

HERO DOWN!

"Look out! He's also got asparagus!" Captain Awesome fell to his knees next to Nacho Cheese Man. "Everyone! Run!"

It didn't take much to make the kids in Ms. Beasley's class run around like crazy people, and a guy dressed as a zebra carrying a tray of steamed vegetables was the only excuse they needed.

"Run before the zucchini gets us!" Dara Sim yelled.

"Ahhh! I'm turning into cauliflower!" Neal Chaykin screamed.

Stan Kirby Jr. ran in circles and just kept yelling, "BOK CHOY! BOK CHOY! BOK CHOY!" as loud as he could.

Meanwhile Meredith just sat silently, arms crossed, glaring at Captain Awesome.

CHAPTER 7

Why DO Giraffes Have Spots?

By
Eugene

After Ms. Beasley's class was offered chocolate milk with elephant straws just to be quiet, lunch was over.

"Okay, who's ready to see the gorillas?" Randy called out.

A chorus of cheers rang out, except for one lone voice that asked, "What about the elephants?"

Randy turned to Eugene. "We'll try to get there, bud, but I can't promise that you'll see much. These elephants don't like crowds," he replied. "Now can anyone tell me what continent gorillas come from?" he asked as they arrived at Gorilla Gulch.

"Africa!" Meredith yelled out without raising her hand.

"There are *elephants* in Africa too!" Eugene added.

"I wish *you* were in Africa!" Meredith snarled.

"And I wish *you* were on the moon!" Eugene replied.

Randy pointed out a big black gorilla sitting next to a tree. "That's a silverback. He's the leader of the troop."

"Okay, that's actually pretty cool," Eugene whispered to Charlie.

"Come on, gang!" Randy called. "Next stop: giraffes! A fully grown giraffe can be as tall as *twenty* feet!"

"A fully grown elephant can use its trunk to reach as high as twenty-*three* feet," Eugene called out.

"That's true, but we're talking about giraffes now," Randy replied.

Eugene imagined what it would be like to have a

neck like a giraffe. He stretched his own neck as high as it would go.

Charlie tapped Eugene on the shoulder and snapped him out of his daydream. "Come on," Charlie said. "We're going to see the tigers!"

ROAR!

"We have three Bengal tigers here at the Sunnyview Memorial Zoo," Randy said as they arrived at the Mall of Tigers. "Bengal tigers live in the wild in India."

"You know what else you can find in the wild in India?" Sally asked.

"Elephants!" Randy replied. "And that brings us to the moment you've all been waiting for . . . and some of you definitely more than others," he added, looking at Eugene. "Next stop is the—"

"ELEPHANTS!" cried Eugene. He turned and raced down the path toward the Elephant Habitat. "MI-TEEEEEEEEEEE!"

"What he said!" Charlie yelled, and ran after Eugene with Sally right beside him.

CHAPTER 8

Elephant
Hide-and-Seek

By
Eugene

ELEPHANT
HABITAT ➡

Finally! The Elephant Habitat!
Huge rocks! Tall trees! A small lake!
It was everything Eugene, Charlie,
and Sally had dreamed it would
be. Except for one very important
thing . . .

"Where are all the elephants?!"
Eugene cried.

"As I said, these elephants can
be a little shy," Randy repeated.

Eugene couldn't believe it. "But

they weigh more than ten thousand pounds! They're more than ten-feet tall! They have twenty-six teeth! What are they shy about?!"

"I can't say I ever asked them," Randy joked.

But Eugene didn't laugh. Neither did Charlie or Sally.

"Look, I'm really sorry," Randy continued. "I wish the elephants would come out so everyone could see them, but one rule we have at the zoo is that we never force the animals to do something they don't want to do. We're almost out of time, but is there any place you'd like to go visit again?"

"Pink Flamingo Pond!" Meredith called out.

BARF!

"You got it," Randy said. "Let's check it out again!"

DOUBLE BARF!

Charlie gasped. "Do you think Randy and Little Miss Stinky Pinky are working together?!" he asked.

"That's even more obvious than the spots on a giraffe,"

Eugene said, shaking his head. "Randy is not a normal employee of the Sunnyview Memorial Zoo. He's the Raging Randonkey, who tries to keep kids from seeing their favorite animals!"

"Of course!" Sally agreed. "Why else would he bail on the elephants?"

"And take the class back to the place only *Meredith* wants to go," Eugene added. "It can't end like this, team! It *can't!*"

"What do we do?" Sally asked.

Eugene knew. "We're going to do what Super Dude would do!"

he replied. "We're going to fight for truth, justice, and our right to see some elephants!"

"SUNNYVIEW SUPERHERO SQUAD, ASSEMBLE!" Eugene, Charlie, and Sally called out in heroic unison.

BACKPACKS! OUTFITS! SUPERHEROES!

"Follow me, guys. Next stop, Pink Flamingo Pond!" Randy said. But Randy never made it to the flamingoes, because his path was suddenly blocked by the World's Most Awesomest Superheroes!

"Whoa, not so fast, Raging Randonkey!" Captain Awesome said, thrusting out his hand like a stop sign. "We're here to save the day . . . *and* this field trip!"

"Well, well, if it isn't Captain

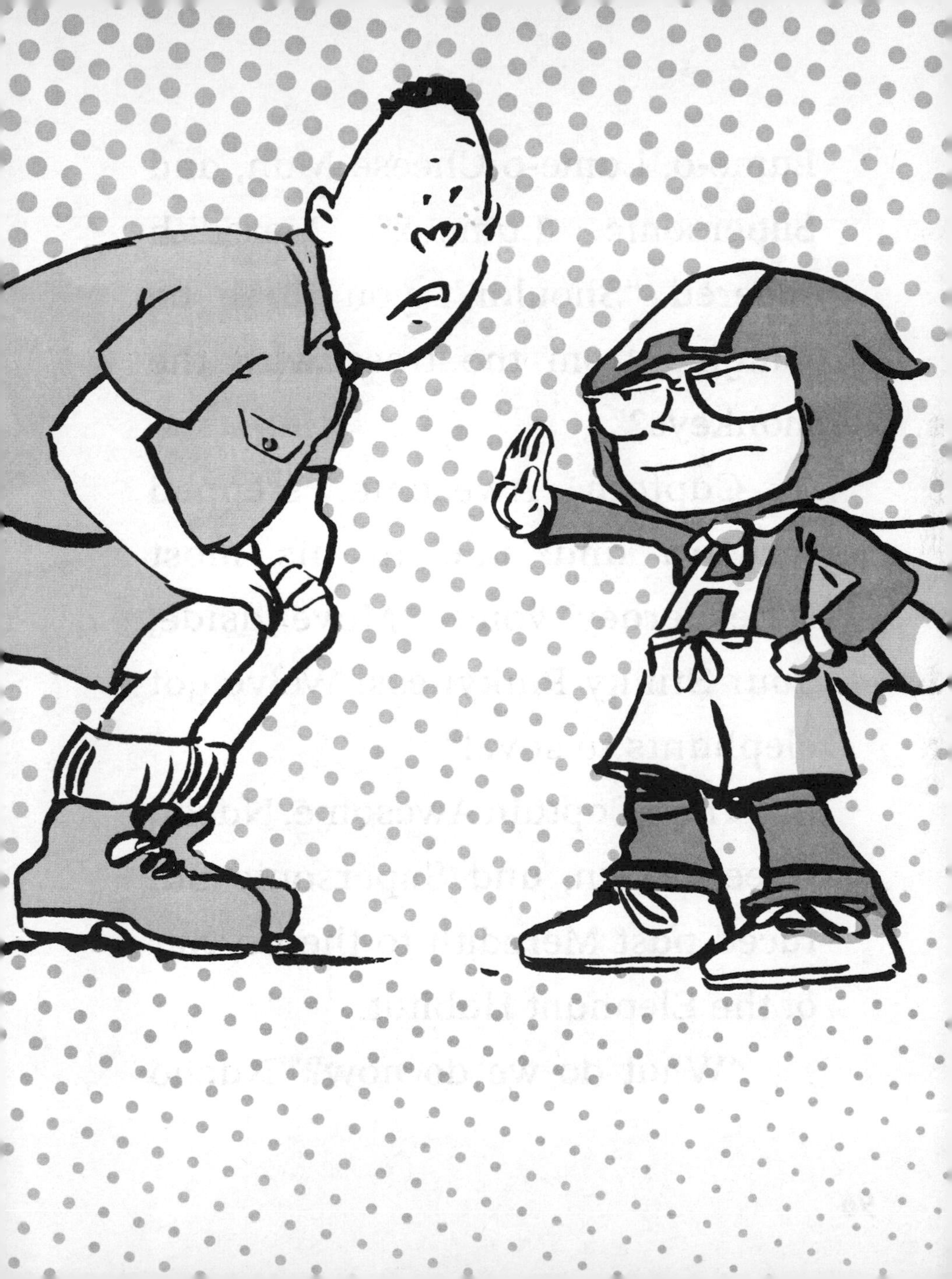

Lame-o, Lame-o Cheese Man, and Supersonic Lame-o," Meredith sneered. "Shouldn't you three be hanging from the trees with the monkeys?"

Captain Awesome stepped forward and said in his most superheroey voice, "Move aside, Your Stinky Pinkyness! We've got elephants to save!"

Then Captain Awesome, Nacho Cheese Man, and Supersonic Sal raced past Meredith to the barrier of the Elephant Habitat.

"What do we do now?" Nacho

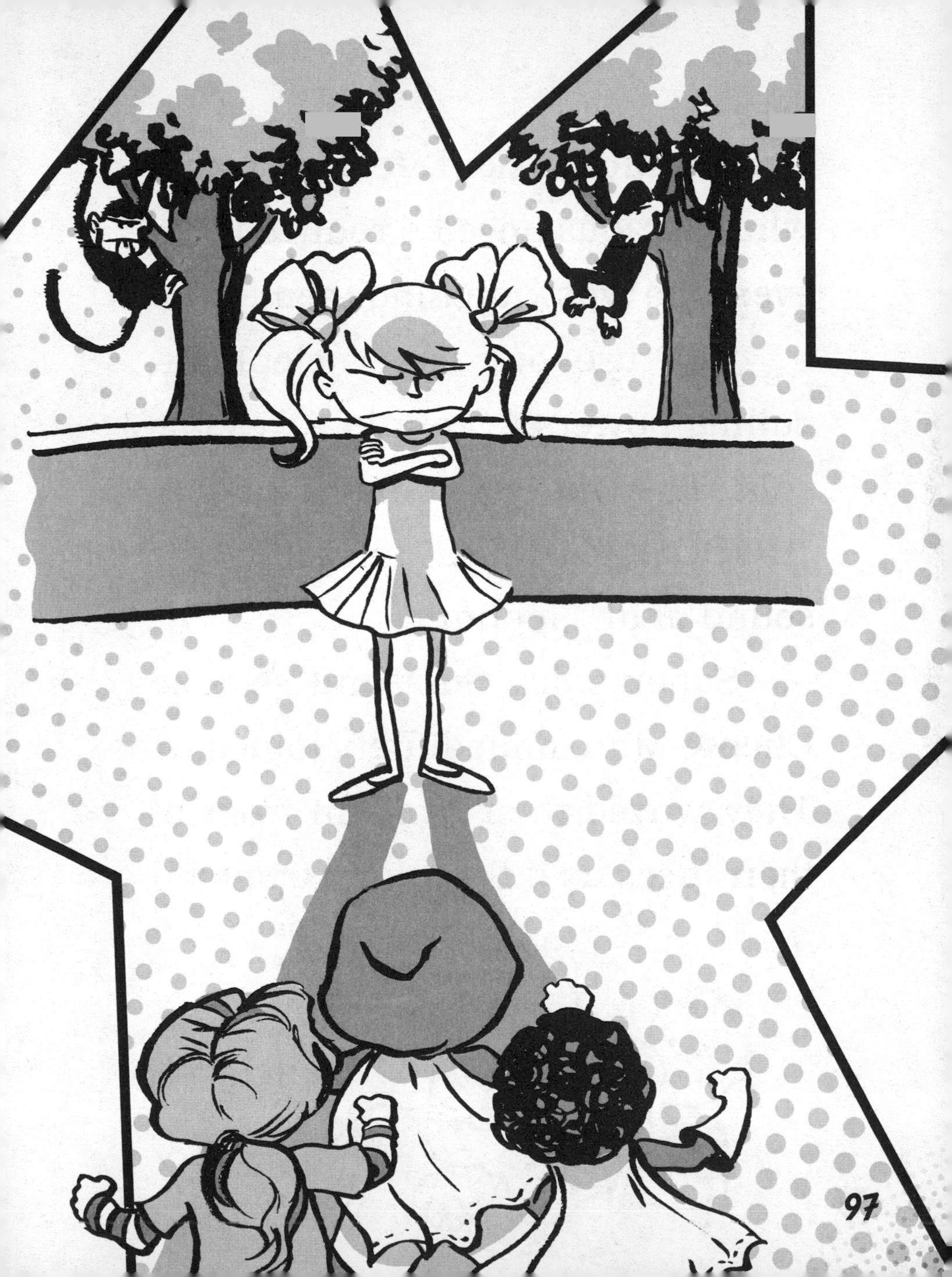

Cheese Man asked, feeling some-
what nervous once he realized that
everyone was watching them.

"We use our super elephant-
calling powers!" Captain Awesome
said. Then he let loose a mighty
"HOOOOOOOONK!" to imitate the
sound of an elephant.

Supersonic Sal and Nacho
Cheese Man immediately joined in.
They waved their arms in front of
their faces as if they were trunks.

"HOOOOOOOONK!"

Other zoo visitors gathered around the Elephant Habitat—not to see the elephants, but to stare at the three strange kids waving their arms like trunks and making elephant noises as loudly as they could.

"HOOOOOOOONK!"

ELEPHANT HABITAT

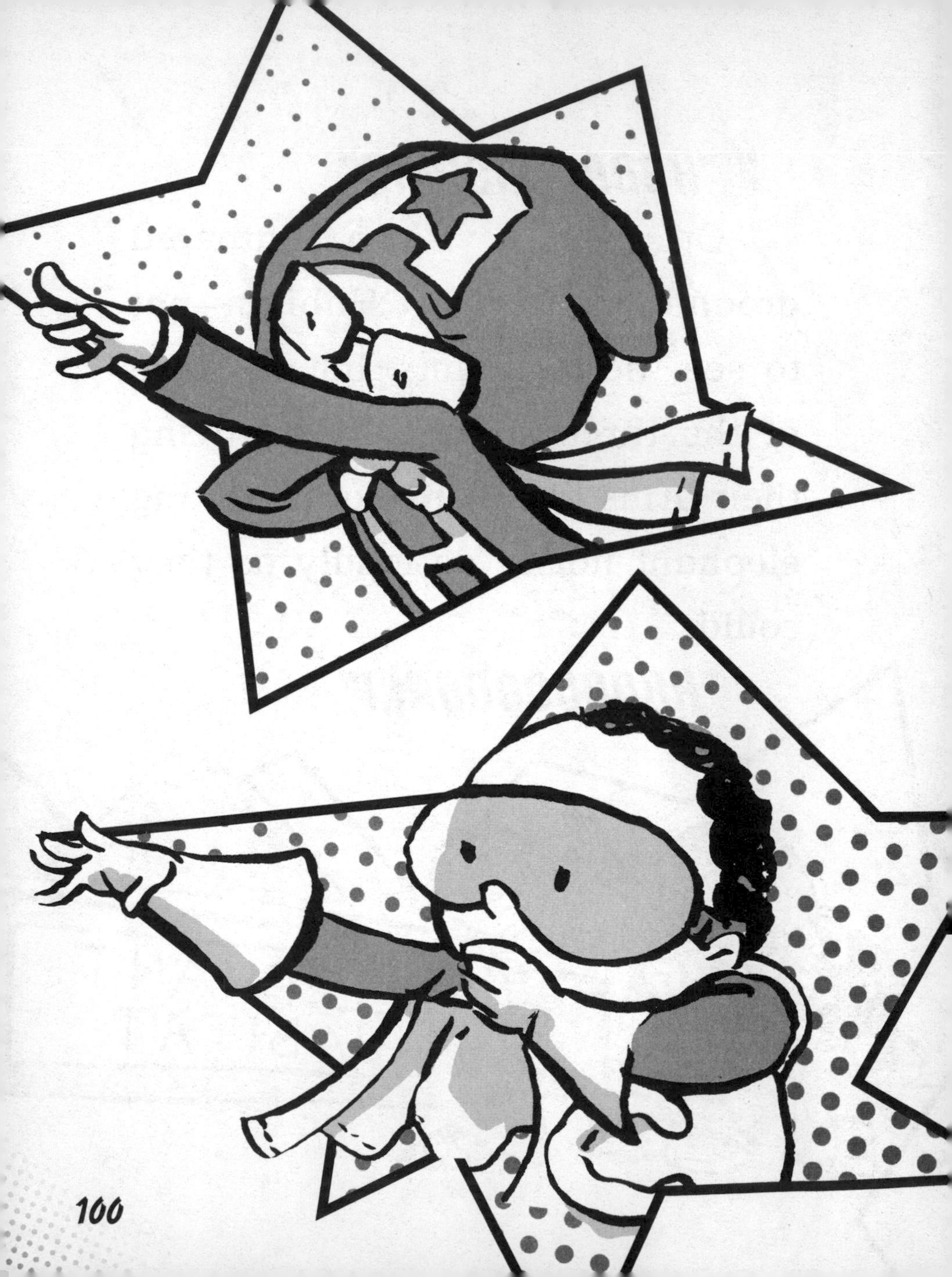

The heroic trio trumpeted at the top of their superlungs and . . . nothing happened. Not a sound in reply. Not a peep. Not a squeak. And certainly not an elephant. Even Ms. Beasley was disappointed.

"I don't think it's going to work," Nacho Cheese Man said with a sad sigh.

"I'm not giving up!" Captain Awesome replied. "Did Super Dude give up when the Vampire Snowman tried to give him a frostbite? Did he quit when the Umpirate called him out at home plate *and* made him walk the plank? No! Super Dude never quits, and neither does Captain Awesome!"

Captain Awesome took a deep superbreath and let out the biggest, mightiest, elephantiest elephant noise anyone had ever heard! **"HOOOOOOOOOOOOOOO-OOOOOOOOOOOOOOOOOOONK!"**

"Well, that was entertaining . . . NOT,"said Meredith. She opened her mouth to let out a huge fake yawn, but it turned into a ginormous gasp instead! "Look!" she shouted.

PEEK!
STARE!

A long, gray trunk appeared from behind a giant boulder! And that trunk was connected to . . . a big, beautiful elephant!

"HOOOOOOOOOOOOOOOOOO OOOONK!" the elephant replied to Captain Awesome.

And then a second elephant appeared, followed by a third and a fourth. One by one the elephants came out until the whole herd stood at the edge of the water and raised their trunks to join Captain Awesome, Nacho Cheese Man, and Supersonic Sal. Then Wilma Eisner started to trumpet. And Olivia Simonson. And

Mike Flinch, Gil Ditko, and Dara Sim. Even Ms. Beasley and the other zoo visitors joined in until it was one big, elephant-trumpeting parade!

Then Randy tried his elephant call too! Maybe he wasn't the Raging Randonkey after all.

"We did it, Captain Awesome! We got the elephants to come out!" Nacho Cheese Man cheered.

He, Supersonic Sal, and Captain Awesome gave one another mighty High Fives of Elephant Victory!

CHAPTER 9

The Total Best Gift of Awesomeness!

By
Eugene

The field trip was almost over. All that was left was a last stop at the zoo gift shop. Eugene wanted to buy presents for his mom and dad . . . and even his little sister, Queen Stinkypants. And that was when he saw it. "Sally! Charlie! Look at this!" Eugene called out.

Sally and Charlie turned to see the most amazing gift *anyone* could ever get: the totally brand-new

Super Dude Zoo Special!

JOY!

It was sixty-four-pages of evil-punching awesomeness! And all for the low price of $5.95!

"I've got one dollar left!" Eugene said.

"I've got three dollars left!" Sally added.

Both kids looked to Charlie in anticipation as he dug through his pockets and pulled out two piles of coins.

"I've got . . . ninety-five cents!" Charlie said.

"That's only four dollars and ninety-five cents!" Eugene said, groaning. "We're one dollar short! How can the forces of good be one dollar short at a time like this?!"

"Don't worry, guys. We've got you covered."

The trio turned to see their classmates holding out coins. Each classmate handed change to Eugene until they got to one dollar.

"We thank Captain Awesome and his friends for a great day," Mike Flinch said.

"Best field trip ever!" Jane Romita agreed.

Eugene, Charlie, and Sally were ready to pay for their Super Dude

Zoo Special, but Randy stepped in to block their way.

"Not so fast, guys," he said.

If it's a fight he wants . . . Eugene thought.

But it wasn't. Instead Randy handed Eugene, Charlie, and Sally their own special elephant pins.

"By the authority of the Sunnyview Memorial Zoo, I hereby declare you: Eugene McGillicudy, Charlie Thomas Jones, and Sally Williams to be Honorary Elephants!"

HOOOOOONK!

It turned out Eugene was wrong about Randy. He *was* a good guy.

The kids were back on the bus within minutes.

Eugene was once again stuck next to Meredith, who was petting the pink stuffed flamingo she had bought at the gift shop.

But Eugene didn't even mind. He, Charlie, and Sally had saved the day, seen the elephants, found a new Super Dude comic, and even become Honorary Elephants. There was only one word to sum up how Eugene felt . . .

MI-TEE!

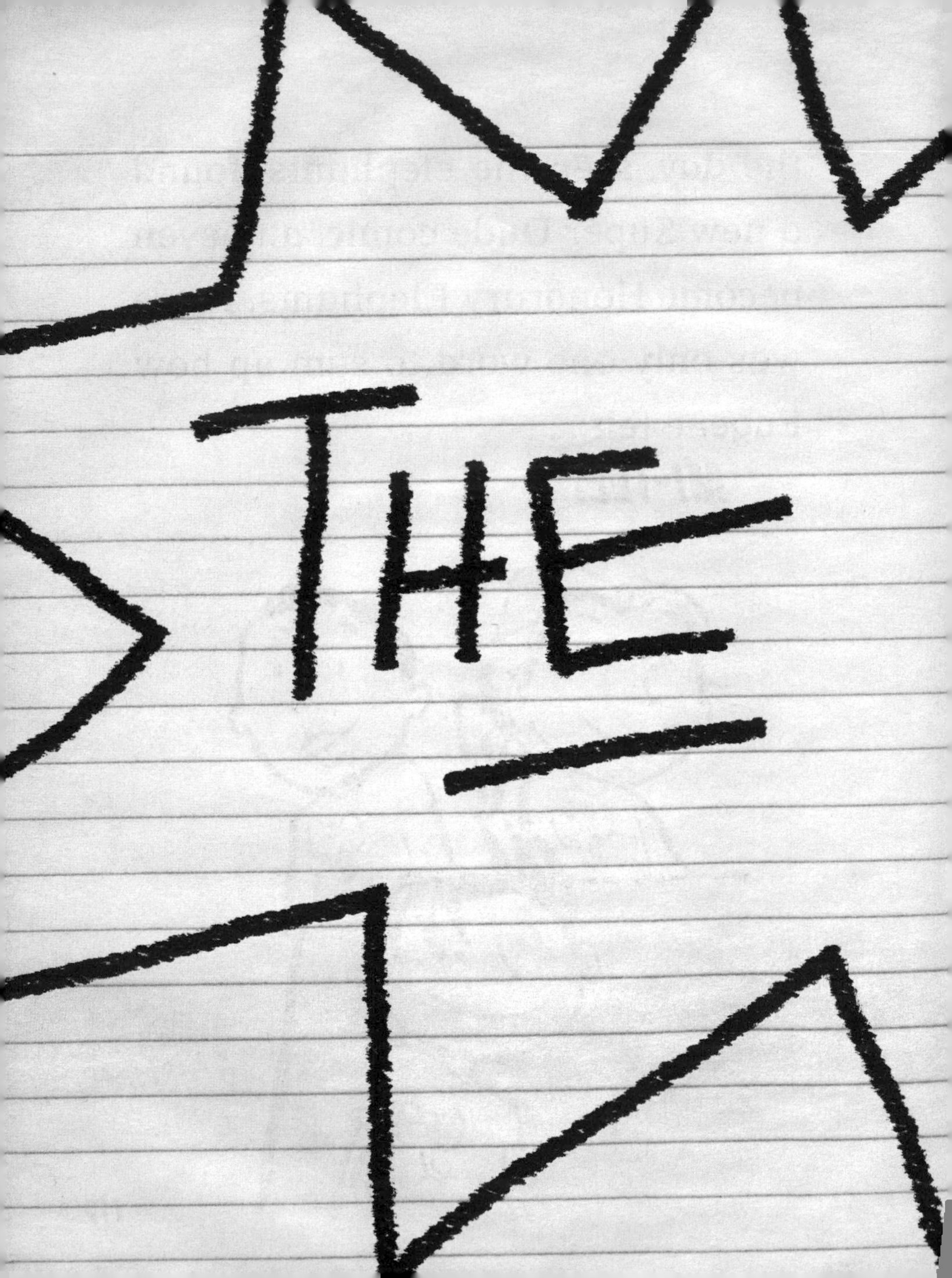
THE

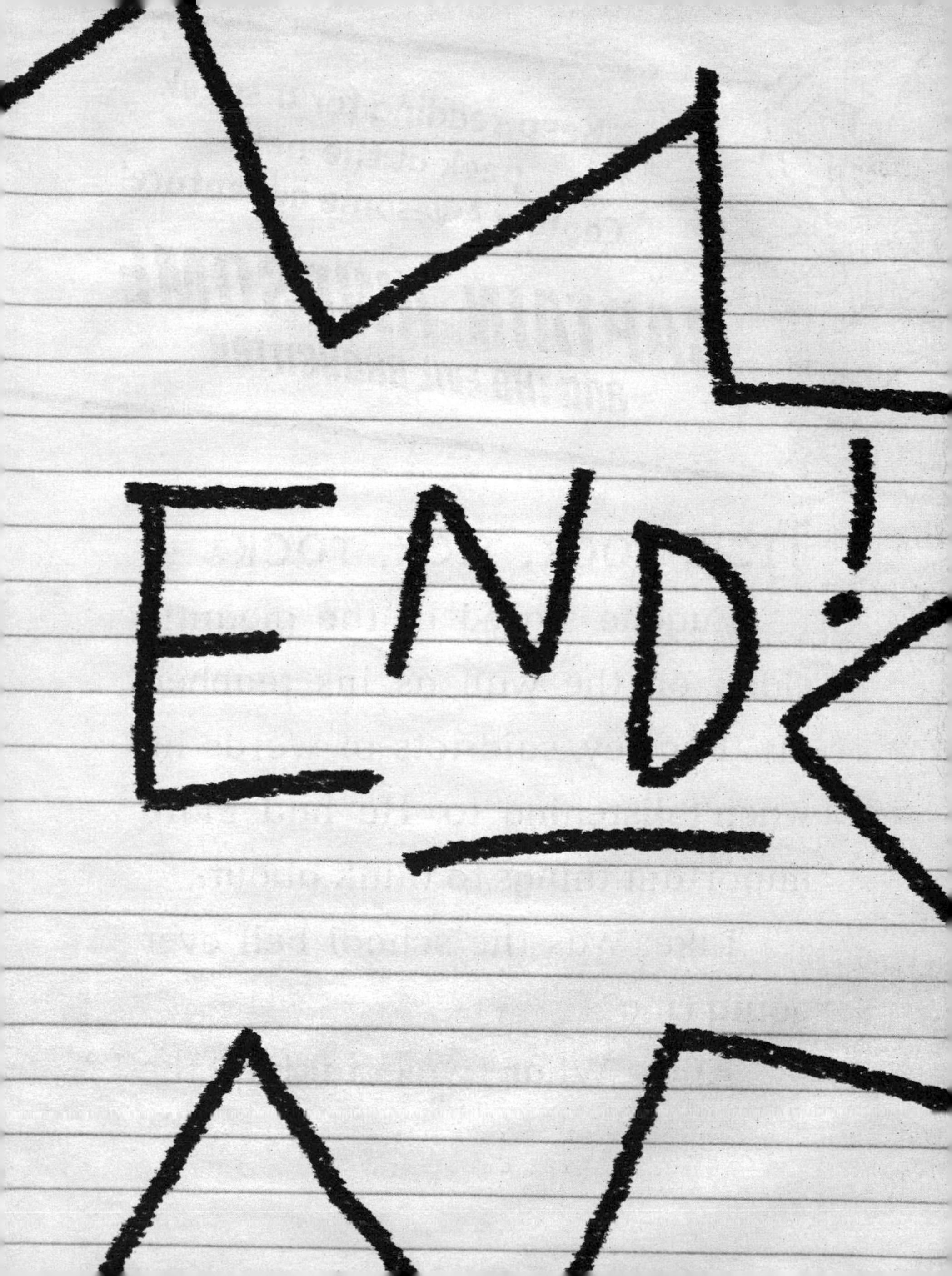
END!

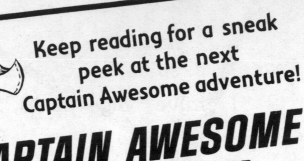

Keep reading for a sneak peek at the next Captain Awesome adventure!

CAPTAIN AWESOME
AND THE EVIL BABYSITTER

TICK, TOCK, TICK, TOCK.

Eugene stared at the gigantic clock on the wall as his teacher, Ms. Beasley, said lots of words he wasn't listening to. He had more important things to think about.

Like: Was the school bell ever going ring?

And: What was taking the

weekend so long to get here?

I have big plans, Eugene thought.

BIG WEEKEND PLANS!

Eugene squirmed in his chair. He could hardly wait. Friday. Saturday. Sunday. Are there any three days that go together better? They're like cake, icing, and sprinkles! They're like popping a balloon and finding it's full of ice cream! They're like, well, you get the idea.

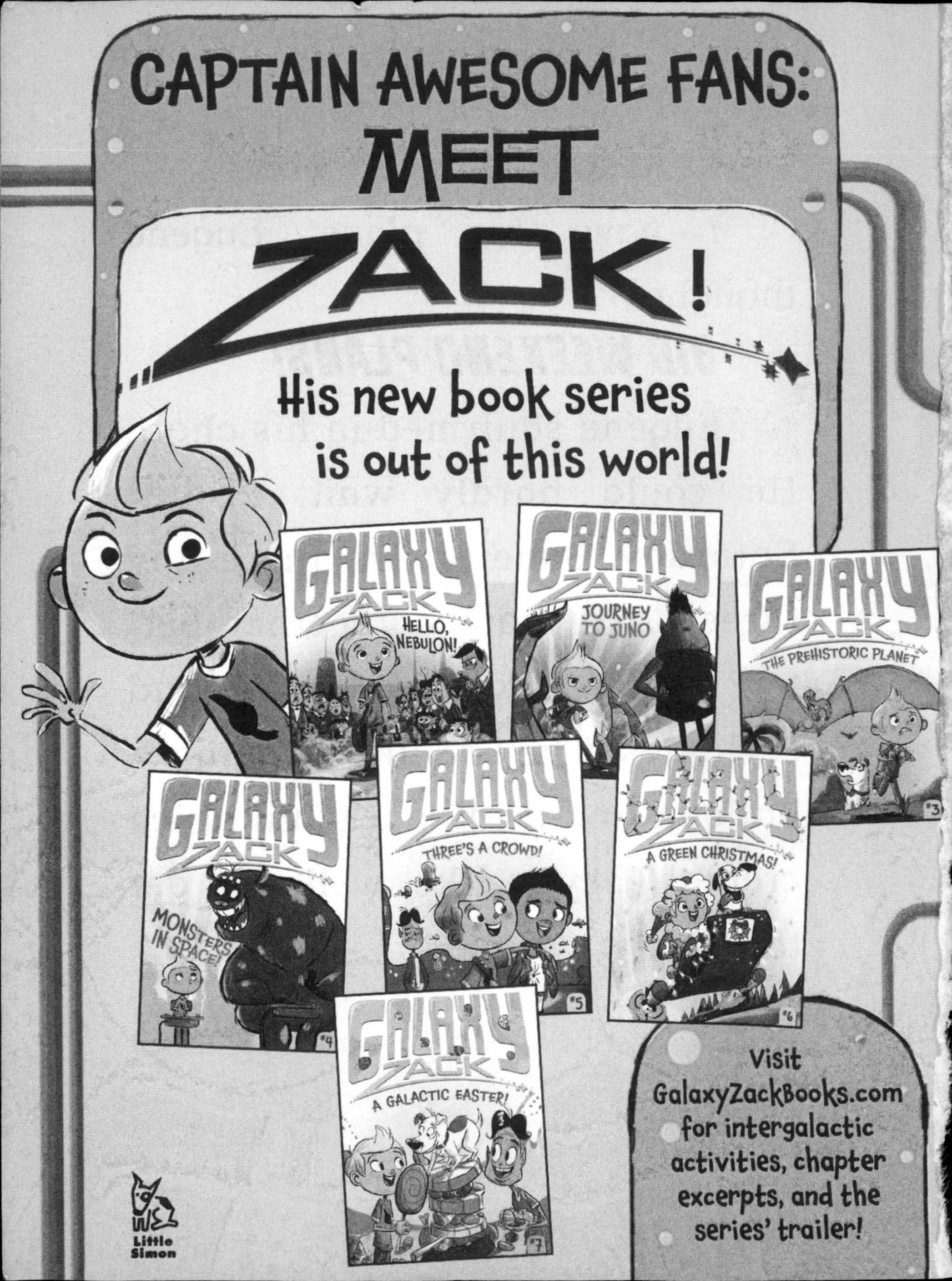
CAPTAIN AWESOME FANS:
MEET
ZACK!
His new book series is out of this world!
GALAXY ZACK
HELLO, NEBULON!
GALAXY ZACK
JOURNEY TO JUNO
GALAXY ZACK
THE PREHISTORIC PLANET
#3
GALAXY ZACK
MONSTERS IN SPACE!
#4
GALAXY ZACK
THREE'S A CROWD!
#5
GALAXY ZACK
A GREEN CHRISTMAS!
#6
GALAXY ZACK
A GALACTIC EASTER!
#7
Little Simon
Visit GalaxyZackBooks.com for intergalactic activities, chapter excerpts, and the series' trailer!